Gym Stars

Dear Reader,

Like Tara in Gym Stars I dreamed of becoming a world-class gymnast and joined my local gym club. Tara's story reminds me of my early days of training and the thrill of entering my first big competition.

I hope you enjoy reading about Tara as much as I have and if you want to become a gym star too – go for it! With focus, talent and dedication your dreams really can come true...
Love,

Beth
Tweddle
X GBR

★ *For Katie* ★

This edition published in the UK in 2016 by Usborne Publishing Ltd., Usborne Publishing Ltd.,
Usborne House, 83-85 Saffron Hill, London EC1N 8RT, England.
www.usborne.com

First published in the UK in 2012.

Copyright © Jane Lawes, 2012

The right of Jane Lawes to be identified as the author
of this work has been asserted by her in accordance with the
Copyright, Designs and Patents Act, 1988.

Cover illustration by Barbara Bongini

The name Usborne and the devices ♡ 🏠 are Trade Marks of
Usborne Publishing Ltd.

A CIP catalogue record for this book is available from the British Library.

JFMA JJASOND/16

ISBN 9781474922951 00667/8

Printed in the UK.

Jane Lawes

Gym Stars

Handsprings and Homework

USBORNE

Dear Reader,

When I was growing up, I used to live, breathe and dream gymnastics – like Tara, I loved working and working on new moves with my coach as I wanted them to look absolutely perfect!

Gymnastics is a fantastic sport, and with hard work and determination, can be extremely rewarding. It can also be very dangerous however, and without the correct supervision and equipment, can easily lead to injury. Because of this, it's so important to make sure that you practise everything in a gym, where you have the right equipment and supervision.

Since these books have been published, I've loved hearing all your stories about new moves you've tried and competitions you've won, and can't wait to hear more! I just wanted to pass on what my coach used to tell me – always make sure that you practise everything in the safe environment of the gym!

Keep trying, keep working and most importantly, be safe!

Lots of love,

www.janelawes.co.uk

Chapter One

Tara Bailey stood in the middle of the springy blue floor at Silverdale Gymnastics Club and shivered. It was her first day back in the gym after Christmas and outside it was icy, but the tingle running down Tara's spine wasn't from the cold. It was a shiver of excitement.

"Ready?" asked Clare, her gymnastics coach. Tara bit her lip and nodded. She was definitely ready. In her mind, she'd been ready to do a backflip for months and months. But actually doing it was something different. She looked down at her feet, positioned neatly together on the floor. She could do backflips – or flicks, as all the gymnasts called them – with support from Clare, but she'd never tried one on her own before.

The last few minutes of the training session were ticking away. It was now or...well, not never...but she wouldn't get another chance until Friday, and two days away from Silverdale Gym *seemed* like for ever.

"Go, Tara!" whooped Megan. Tara grinned down at the floor. The other members of her Acrobatic Gymnastics group knew how desperate she was to do a flick by herself. She'd hardly talked about anything else since Regionals two months ago – the first gymnastics competition she'd ever taken part in. Not only had she won her first ever gold medal, but Tara and her partner Lindsay had also won the chance to compete in the National Acro competition for their level in a few months' time. Tara still couldn't believe it... and she was training harder than ever to make sure she was ready.

Standing very still, with her arms held by her sides, she prepared to try her first unassisted backflip. She kept her legs straight and leaned her weight back until she felt like she was about to topple over. Then she swung her arms up and pushed herself backwards, off the floor and onto her hands. Another push with her hands, and she was back on her feet again. Tara could hardly believe what had happened. She'd done a backflip without support, and she hadn't even landed on her head!

"Well done!" said Clare. "It was messy, but it's there. Work on keeping your legs together."

Tara nodded, breathless. It had been so quick that she hadn't had time to think about being neat or any of the things she remembered to do when she practised on the trampoline. She tried once more and got all the way over again. But her legs would not stay stuck together like she wanted, and Clare said her knees were bent.

"Brilliant," whispered Lindsay, as their coach went off to help Megan and Sophie practise punch-front somersaults. "Clare's just being picky."

"No, she's right," Tara replied. "I've got to keep practising until my flicks are better. Just getting over isn't enough." But she smiled at Lindsay to show that she didn't mind Clare's criticism, and she felt secretly pleased that Lindsay thought she'd done well. Besides, she'd managed two flicks in a row for the first time – nothing could ruin her day now.

They watched Megan and Sophie, two older girls in their group. Tara couldn't help feeling a bit jealous when she saw them take a run-up, jump onto both feet and whip their bodies round in tucked somersaults. One day, she promised herself…one day she'd be doing that, too.

"That's enough for today," Clare said to Sophie,

and Tara looked over her shoulder at the clock high up on the wall. The hands had reached six o'clock and training was over.

"Nationals gymnasts!" Clare shouted, as the group began to leave the gym. "I want to talk to you before you go."

Tara still felt butterflies in her stomach every time she remembered that she was one of the Nationals gymnasts. Megan and Sophie were going to the Nationals too, as well as Jasmine and Sam, the most advanced girls in their squad.

"Your routines looked great at Regionals," Clare began, when they'd settled themselves on the floor. "You've had a bit of a break over Christmas, so I hope you've all recovered from the competition and are ready to work hard again! I'm glad to see that most of you have kept up with your stretching, even when you weren't at the gym." Clare paused and looked directly at Megan, who had complained more than anyone about being stiff during their first session back.

"It's important that you do at least a little bit when you have time off."

Tara caught Megan's eye and exchanged a sympathetic grimace with her. During the week away from Silverdale, she'd loved being able to relax and spend more time with her best friends from school, Emily and Kate. But after a few afternoons watching Christmas films she'd missed the gym, and she'd made a big effort to do half an hour of stretching at home every day. She hoped she'd still be able to fit it in when she went back to school.

"There'll be extra training sessions for the National competition, just like there were for Regionals," continued Clare. "They'll start again this Sunday at 9 a.m. I'd like all of you to get working on some new balances for your routines."

Excitement rippled around the group and Tara hugged her knees into her chest. Learning new balances was so exciting! In Acrobatic Gymnastics, gymnasts performed routines in pairs and groups of three or four. They had to do balances as well as floor skills like backflips and somersaults. Tara had only been doing Acro for half a year, but balances had quickly become her favourite challenge.

Now all her dreams were made up of spectacular routines full of things she'd seen the more experienced gymnasts at Silverdale doing – breathtaking balances and amazing throws and somersaults that she and Lindsay would learn to do sometime in the far-off future. Instead of imagining what it would be like to be a famous singer or a glamorous actress like her school friends sometimes did, she dreamed of being a famous gymnast like Beth Tweddle.

"Wow, my legs ache *so* much," groaned Sophie, when they'd wrapped themselves up in coats, scarves and gloves, and were walking out to the car park.

"Mine too," agreed Megan. "It was nice to have time off for Christmas, but we're paying for it now."

"We'll get used to it again soon," said Lindsay. "Especially with the extra training for Nationals."

"Wednesdays, Fridays, Saturdays, and now Sundays too – if Clare had her own way we'd be in the gym every day!" said Megan.

"All day, every day," laughed Sophie.

"That would be so much better than school," Tara said, smiling as she imagined it. Nothing but gymnastics – it sounded like heaven.

Chapter Two

On Saturday morning, Tara woke up to discover that while she'd been asleep, a glittering blanket of pure white snow had covered the whole town.

"It's so white!" gasped Anna, her little sister, who had been looking forward to snow for months and months.

"Will we be able to get to the gym?" Tara asked Dad anxiously, peering out of the window at the icy road.

"We'll soon find out," Dad replied cheerfully. "Wellies on, Anna, if you're going outside."

Anna hopped around, trying to pull her second welly boot on. Tara sat on the bottom stair, watching her. She already had her shoes and coat on, and her gym bag at her side. She'd been ready for ages, knowing that it might take longer than usual to get to Silverdale.

"Shouldn't we leave soon?" she asked. "We'll have to drive really slowly because of the snow."

"In a minute," said Dad. "I've got to scrape ice off the car windows first."

"We'll help," said Tara. This was progress, at least. "Won't we, Anna?"

"I'm making a snowman," declared Anna, and ran out to the back garden.

"Sure you don't want to stay home and help with the snowman?" Dad asked Tara.

"No," she said firmly. "I want to go to the gym!"

"Okay, okay," laughed Dad. "Just checking!"

There was a layer of snow on top of the car that looked like thick white icing on a Christmas cake. It took ages to scrape the windows clear and by the time they'd finished, Tara's fingers felt frozen, even though she was wearing gloves. She jumped into the passenger seat.

"Let's go!" She looked at her watch. If they left now, they'd still have enough time to get there before training started.

But the car wouldn't start. Tara groaned and leaned her head back against the seat. Dad tried again. On the fifth try, the car rumbled to life. Tara and Dad grinned at each other.

"Silverdale, here we come!" cried Dad. He reversed the car slowly out of the drive. Tara felt the wheels slip on the ice. She looked across at Dad. He was gripping the steering wheel so tightly that his knuckles were bony and white. He inched around a tiny bit and the car slipped again. He pulled the car up to the kerb and stopped.

"I'm sorry, Tara," he said. "This road's like an ice rink. It's too dangerous."

"That's okay," Tara mumbled.

"Never mind, eh?" said Dad, undoing his seat belt. "You can help us with the snowman now!"

"Great," Tara said flatly.

When she got back inside, she phoned Silverdale and spoke to Clare.

"I'm really sorry," she said, when she'd explained.

"Don't be silly," said Clare. "I don't want you getting hurt trying to get here. Anyway, you're not the only one. Sophie and Jack are both snowed in, too."

That made her feel a little better, but she couldn't forget that she was letting Lindsay down by missing a whole training session, just when they needed all the practice they could get. During their Friday session, the others had told Tara all about what the Nationals had been like in previous years and how high the standard would be. She felt thrilled to be taking part, but she was also scared that she and Lindsay would look rubbish compared to the other gymnasts competing. They only had two and a half months to make their routine perfect. Now it was two and a half months minus one day!

"Tara!" shrieked Anna, tumbling through the back door. Her cheeks were bright pink and her brown hair had snowflakes stuck in it. "Come and see my snowman. You can help me finish it!"

Tara couldn't help smiling. She put her coat and gloves back on and grabbed her wellies.

"Shout if you need my help," said Dad. He was making a cup of tea for Mum, who was in bed with a horrible cold.

"Okay," said Tara, following her sister outside.

Anna had rolled snow into one giant snowball and one smaller one. "Can you put the head on?" she asked Tara.

"Sure," Tara said, bending down to pick up the smaller ball of snow. It had leaves and grass stuck in it, so she turned that side to face the back. It wasn't too heavy, but Anna was only six so she couldn't have reached. Tara held the head in place on top of the giant snowball, while Anna stretched up to pat handfuls of snow all around to stick it on properly.

"It's good, isn't it?" Anna said, standing back to look at it.

"It's great," Tara agreed. "I'll go get a scarf for him. You find some stones for eyes."

When she came back outside with one of Mum's old scarves, Tara couldn't see Anna anywhere.

"Anna?" she called. "Where are you?"

"Here!" screeched Anna as a snowball hit Tara right between her shoulder blades. Anna might have been small, but she could really throw a snowball.

Tara let out a sound that was half a scream and half laughter, and ran to get some snow off the bushes. The battle was on!

Handsprings and Homework

Later, to give Mum a bit of peace, Dad took Tara and Anna for a snowy walk in the park. On the way they stopped at Emily's, who came out to join them with her two little brothers. Adam was in the same class as Anna at school, and they pelted each other with snowballs all around the park, until one accidentally got Luke, Emily's youngest brother, on the head and he burst into tears.

When Emily had finished fussing over Luke, and he had finally stopped crying, Anna, Adam and Dad carried on with the snowball fight. Tara and Emily wandered along behind them, swishing their feet through the snow and chatting while keeping an eye on three-year-old Luke, who was running along with the others.

"I can't believe we go back to school on Tuesday," said Emily. "The Christmas holidays went so fast!"

"I know," Tara said. "I'm kind of looking

forward to it, though. I haven't seen anyone from our year during the holidays except you and Kate."

"Me too," said Emily. "But I'm not looking forward to all the homework!"

Tara laughed and kicked at some snow. "Don't remind me! I've still got a bit of holiday homework to do."

Emily pulled a face in sympathy. "If you've finished by tomorrow evening, come round to mine and watch a film," she suggested.

"Definitely," agreed Tara, and she decided she would start on the last piece of homework as soon as she got back from the park. Last term, she'd spent so much time training for Regionals that she'd hardly got to see her friends. Tara, Kate and Emily had been in the same class all the way through junior school, but now that they were at secondary school, they were all in different forms and hardly had any lessons together. They tried to make sure they always watched a film together on Sunday evenings, but Tara had missed out a few times because of training for the competition. They'd had arguments and tears, and she'd been so afraid that she was about to lose her best friends. She looked at Emily and felt a rush of determination that it would never happen again.

They were catching up with the others, who had stopped to roll more snowballs. Emily nudged Tara and pointed at Anna, who was sneakily putting snow in the hood of Dad's coat, while he was crouching down to help Luke with a snowball.

"Hi, Dad!" laughed Anna, then tipped the hood over his head. Dad jumped up and grabbed his younger daughter, swinging her high into the air and tickling her. Anna screamed and laughed at the same time. Tara and Emily hovered, giggling, at the edge of the group. One of Anna's pink wellies fell off while Dad held her over his shoulder. He winked at Tara and gave her a secret signal to fill Anna's welly with snow. Tara darted forward, still giggling, and scooped snow into the boot with her gloved hand.

"Here's your welly, Anna," she said, through bursts of laughter, when Dad finally put Anna down. Anna balanced on one foot and reached for the welly Tara held out to her. She shoved her foot in, and the look on her face when she felt the cold, sloppy snow soaking into her sock made Tara collapse against Emily, laughing so much she could hardly stand up.

"Yuck!" screeched Anna. "*Tara!*" She took the welly off again and tipped it upside down so the snow fell out.

"That's what you get for messing with me," Dad said, grinning.

"My foot's wet." Anna pouted.

"Here," said Dad, pulling a spare pair of socks out of his coat pocket. "Put these on instead." Anna hopped over and held his arm for balance while she pulled off the wet sock and changed it for a dry one. She stuck her tongue out at Tara, who was wiping tears of laughter away from her eyes. "It's probably time we went home," said Dad. "Let's go and see if Mum's feeling any better."

They walked Emily, Adam and Luke home, then said goodbye. The ice on the roads had melted, Tara noticed. They could get to Silverdale now, no problem, but her training session had finished. She realized she hadn't really thought about it all day – she'd been too busy enjoying herself. And she didn't think that even gymnastics would have been as much fun.

Mum was feeling a bit better when they got home, and Anna sat on the sofa with her, telling tales on Dad and Tara. Tara could see that Mum was trying not to laugh.

"All ready for school next week?" Dad asked Tara, changing the subject. "New term, lots of new things to learn. I bet you can't wait."

Tara rolled her eyes at his joke, but she *was* kind of looking forward to a new term and a new start. It had been difficult to adjust to secondary school last term, but she hoped that things would be better this time and she'd find a way to cope with the work and gymnastics training, *and* spend more time with her best friends.

"Have you got any homework left to do?" Mum asked.

"A little bit," Tara answered. "I'm going to do it now."

Mum smiled. "Good. Come and show me if you need any help."

"Thanks," said Tara. She went upstairs and got out her maths book. Even though she'd been given the maths homework before Christmas, she still hadn't done it. She'd meant to, right at the start of the holidays, but there always seemed to be something more fun to do and, anyway, she didn't think the questions would take *that* long to do...

She sat at the little desk in her room, chewing the end of her pen, and wondering if she'd be able to get to Silverdale for the extra competition practice the next morning. She hoped the roads stayed clear overnight. Then she switched into school mode, opened her maths book, and tried to get on with it. The questions weren't hard but they took longer than she'd thought, especially because she kept thinking about getting started on the new routine at the gym. She'd be performing it at the Nationals, a bigger competition than she'd ever dreamed of, so it was going to have to be really good.

Eventually she finished the maths questions, then she stood up and looked out of the window. Most of the snow had melted. Anna's snowman was still there, but no new snow had fallen. *Good*, Tara thought. Now she just needed it to hold off tonight.

Chapter Three

The next day, Tara ran downstairs to look out of the front window as soon as she woke up. The roads were clear, and she was relieved. That morning was the first of the special training sessions for the Nationals and she just couldn't miss it.

She nagged Dad so much about getting her to the gym on time that she ended up arriving at Silverdale really early. She'd never been the first one there before. Without all the noise of gymnasts working on the bars, trampolines and the tumbling track, and with no chatter in the changing rooms, it was like a different place.

Soon other gymnasts of all ages began to bustle through the doors, and it wasn't long before Silverdale was as buzzing as ever. Most of the Sunday morning groups, taught by other coaches, did Artistic Gymnastics, working on the beam, bars, floor and vault, and Tara enjoyed catching glimpses of them while her Acro group worked on one of the floor areas. It felt good to be at Silverdale on a Sunday morning again.

Tara waited impatiently in the changing room for Lindsay to arrive, and started to worry that her road might still be too icy for her to come. If her partner didn't get here, there wouldn't be much point in an extra training session. After missing out on a whole two hours of gymnastics the day before, Tara was desperate to make the most of this morning. Just as she was beginning to give up hope, Lindsay rushed in.

"You made it!" cried Tara, her face lighting up.

"I wouldn't miss this for anything," replied Lindsay. "We're training for a National competition, you know."

Tara grinned. "Really? I'd almost forgotten."

Lindsay smiled back, and tugged her T-shirt over her head. She had an emerald green and black leotard on underneath. The dark colours made her long blonde hair look even lighter.

Tara was wearing her Silverdale tracksuit top over her own leotard. She'd been given an official club tracksuit and leotard for the Regional competition. She'd only worn the leotard once so far, to compete at Regionals, but she wore the tracksuit to keep warm at the beginning of most training sessions. She loved the navy blue and white top, which said *Silverdale Gymnastics Club* on the back in white letters. She felt like a real gymnast whenever she wore it. Now she unzipped it, and shivered in the cold of the changing room. "Let's go in and start warming up," she suggested.

Handsprings and Homework

For once, all the gymnasts were glad of the ten laps round the floor that Clare made them run at the beginning of the session. It was the best way to get warm.

"Your leotard matches the weather," Megan said to Tara, when they were sitting in the splits at the end of the warm-up.

"And the temperature in here," joked Lindsay. Tara looked down at the leotard Mum and Dad had given her for Christmas. The body was ice blue and velvety, and it had long white sleeves made of a shiny material. Around the neck, shiny white shapes spiked down like icicles.

When they were fully warmed up, they got to work. Clare asked each pair to go through their routines from Regionals again. Tara wished they could just start learning all the new things for Nationals, but she gritted her teeth and got on with it. Everything in gymnastics took a lot of work and a lot of time.

"Your routines for the Nationals will follow the

same basic choreography," Clare explained, "but we're going to use the next two and a half months to make them much better than they were at Regionals. Some of those extra points will come from the new balances and more difficult gymnastics skills I talked about on Friday. But a lot of them are going to come from practice, practice, practice!"

Eventually, Clare sent them off to a corner of the floor where they could work on balances by themselves, while she watched Megan and Sophie go through their Regionals routine again. When Tara and Lindsay had gone through all the balances they could do, they decided to work on backflips. Clare hadn't put one in their routine yet, because Tara had only just managed them on her own.

"Do you think Clare will let us put backflips in our routine?" Tara asked Lindsay.

"I don't know." Lindsay frowned. "I wish she would, but you've only just learned how to do them. It might be a risk."

Handsprings and Homework

"We're not showing up at Nationals without a backflip in our routine," Tara said determinedly. "Without it, we'll never get near the medals!"

She glanced over at Jasmine and Sam, who were working hard on an amazing new balance. "I can't wait until Clare gets us started on *our* new balances!" she said, grinning. But beneath her excitement, she couldn't help wishing she'd started gymnastics when she was three or four, like Jasmine and Sam. They were competing in Level 4 at the Nationals, while Megan and Sophie were Level 3 gymnasts. Tara sometimes felt far behind them competing at Level 2. She'd learned such a lot since starting at Silverdale last summer, but it wasn't enough. She was desperate to be able to do the things that Jasmine and Sam could do. Jasmine was tiny for a fourteen year old, and Sam, the oldest girl in their group, was really strong. That, and the fact that they'd both been doing Acro almost their whole lives, meant they were the stars of Clare's group. Tara dreamed of catching up and one day being as brilliant as them.

That evening, Tara went over to Emily's to watch a film. She sat on the sofa in between Emily and Kate, her two best friends in the world. Kate had forgotten to bring the DVD she'd been given for Christmas and which she'd promised they would watch, so they'd picked the first *Harry Potter* film instead. Tara felt like she really understood how Harry, Ron and Hermione felt, starting at a big, scary new school. Even though she'd got used to secondary school a bit, she still sometimes felt very small when she was surrounded by all the older girls and boys. And, of course, everything was different to how life had been at junior school. Maybe not *quite* as different as school life was for the characters on the screen, but it was strange to have a different teacher for every lesson, and they were given so much more homework than they'd ever had in Year Six!

Handsprings and Homework

"I wish we could learn spells and magic for homework," said Kate.

"School would be much more fun if we got to learn how to fly a broomstick," agreed Emily.

"In my perfect school, every lesson would be gymnastics, and the only homework would be stretching and practising balances," Tara said, smiling as she nibbled a Christmas biscuit. Emily's parents ran a bakery, and they lived above it. One of the brilliant things about watching Sunday night films at Emily's was that there were always a few leftover biscuits or cakes from the shop, especially at Christmas time. On the table in front of them was a plate full of gingerbread men and Christmas-tree cookies. Emily reached for a gingerbread man and bit one of its feet off.

"Oh, I don't want to go back to school," sighed Kate. "It's so tiring and the holidays have been so much fun!"

"Me neither," said Tara. "I hope we don't get too much homework this term. I won't have time for stupid maths and boring geography – I've got the Nationals coming up!" She noticed an anxious look on Emily's face. "Don't worry, Em," she said. "There's no way I'm letting gymnastics come between us again."

"There's no way we'll let you," said Kate, and Emily smiled.

There was a pause while they all watched an exciting part of the film. Then:

"The holidays were great, but it'll be good to get back to normal," admitted Tara.

"Back to gymnastics, you mean," said Emily, with a grin.

Tara laughed and nodded. Her friends knew her so well.

Chapter Four

The three friends met at the school gate on Tuesday morning.

"Here we are again," grumbled Kate. She yawned and pulled her coat tighter around her. "It was so hard to get up this morning!"

Groups of older girls and boys pushed past them, shouting and laughing. *It is just like the beginning of the autumn term*, Tara thought. She'd felt small and completely lost then, a new girl at a big, noisy school. Now that she and her friends were starting their second term here, she hoped that things might get a bit easier. It was sort of comforting to be going back to the same form room, where there'd be familiar faces all around her, and the same old maps and geography posters on the walls. She only wished that Kate and Emily would be there too; she still hated the fact that all three of them were in different forms.

They hurried off to registration, and then on to their first lessons. *History first thing is a good start to the term*, Tara thought. They were starting a new topic and Mr. Bruce, her teacher, always made everything interesting and fun. This term they were going to be learning about castles, and Tara hoped they'd get a good school trip out of it.

As usual, Mr. Bruce split the class up into groups. Tara's group passed around the pictures of castles they'd been given and pointed at some of the features Mr. Bruce had talked about. But after a minute or two, everyone was chatting about the Christmas break. Tara hadn't seen anyone in her history class during the holidays and it was fun hearing about all the things they'd got up to.

"We had a massive snowball fight on my road," said Matt. "The kids from all the houses came out and we had two big teams – girls against boys."

"Who won?" asked Tara.

"The girls, *obviously*," said Natalie, who lived on Matt's road.

"Only because there were way more of you!" cried Matt.

Tara and the others in the group laughed and someone else started a story about a New Year's Eve party. Tara thought about the most exciting things she'd done in the holidays…but she didn't think anyone would want to hear about learning to do a backflip.

At the end of the lesson, Mr. Bruce asked them to research one type of castle. Tara scribbled the instructions down in her homework diary.

She didn't mind doing that kind of homework; she thought it might be really interesting.

If only the homework had stopped there. Tara had science after history, which was nice because it meant she got to sit next to Emily, but which also meant another piece of homework. Then art was after break. Tara didn't enjoy art. She wished she could draw like Emily, or come up with good ideas like Kate, but she could never make her paintbrush paint what she wanted it to, and things never turned out how she imagined they would. In junior school, art had been one of her favourite lessons, but now it was hard work. Their teacher seemed to think that the homework she gave them would be great fun, but Tara knew that researching the painter they'd be learning about was going to take ages.

After lunch, the three friends finally had a lesson all together: maths.

"I have *so* much homework already," sighed Kate, leaning against the wall in the corridor, while they waited for the class before them to leave the maths room.

"Me too," Emily and Tara said at the same time.

"And it's only the first day back!" continued Kate.

"Let's hope Mr. Spencer doesn't give us another four pages of maths questions like he did for the holidays," said Emily.

"That would be too mean!" said Kate, with a look of horror.

Tara laughed at Kate's expression, but inside she was seriously worried. She already had so much to do that she couldn't possibly do it all tonight. That meant she'd have to leave some until tomorrow, but she had gym after school on Wednesdays, so she wouldn't be able to get *anything* done then. Her mind was spinning as she tried to work out when she was going to do everything.

She felt a prod in her back and realized that her class were going in. As she took her usual seat in the front row, Kate and Emily trudged past to their seats together at the back, and Tara thought, as she always did, that having to sit in alphabetical order was really unfair. She watched the rest of the class come in and settle down. Everyone seemed really tired. She hoped Mr. Spencer would take pity on them and make the lesson easy.

They escaped from maths with only a few questions for homework, and then it was just music left. Tara sank into her seat in the music room with relief. At least she knew there'd be no homework from this class. She looked at the things she'd already written in her homework diary and tried to work out what she might get asked to do tomorrow. She flicked the book shut and put it away. *It would all get done somehow*, she thought. She just wasn't going to think about when.

Chapter Five

Tara tried to start on her homework as soon as she got home from school that evening, but even though it was only the first day back she was really tired after a full day of lessons. After dinner she did more homework, but she wasn't anywhere near finished when her eyelids began to feel heavy, and she had to stop and go to bed before she'd got everything done.

It felt like the only time Tara wasn't doing stuff

for school was when she was at the gym. And, of course, evenings at the gym meant that no homework got done at all – by the time she'd got home and had dinner, she was so tired that all she could do was shower away the day's hard work and crawl into bed.

On Wednesday and Friday, she and Lindsay worked on their old balances at Silverdale, making sure they were as perfect as they could be.

"I think it's time for you two to start learning a new balance for your routine," Clare finally said on Saturday morning. Tara was going to learn to do a straddle lever on Lindsay's hands. Clare asked Jasmine and Sam to demonstrate how it worked and what it should look like, which was amazing! Tara watched Jasmine's movements closely, hoping to pick up some tips to get it right. Then she and Lindsay tried it themselves.

Lindsay had to lie on her back with her feet planted on the floor so that her knees pointed to the ceiling. She held her arms up to the ceiling, too, with her hands flat, palms facing upwards. Tara stood behind Lindsay's head and pressed her own hands down onto Lindsay's. Then she had to take her feet off the floor, one at a time, and stretch her legs out diagonally in front of her into a straddle lever position, as if she was sitting on the floor with her legs out to the sides, but actually balancing in the air on Lindsay's hands. Tara knew that if they could do it, it would look brilliant. She understood what she had to do, and she could see it perfectly in her mind. The problem was, she couldn't actually manage it. She couldn't even hold herself off the floor long enough to straighten her legs, never mind hold a straddle lever for a whole four seconds. It was the beginning of January and the competition was in the middle of March. A million years wouldn't be long enough to learn this balance, she thought – two and a half months definitely wasn't enough time.

"Don't worry," said Clare, seeing the crushed look on Tara's face. "You need to build up strength in your arms and legs. Then you'll find it much easier."

"How am I going to do that?" asked Tara.

"Wait here," said Clare, with a mysterious smile.

Tara looked at Lindsay and shrugged.

"Try using this," said their coach, returning with a piece of equipment Tara had seen Jasmine using sometimes. It was two wooden blocks, each about the size of an adult's hand. Each block was stuck on the top of a long rectangular block. These were standing upright on a flat wooden board, and they were about as far apart as Lindsay's hands would be when Tara balanced on them. The whole thing came up to above her knees.

She put her hands on the blocks, which felt much sturdier than Lindsay's hands, and lifted one leg off the ground so that her knee was bent and pointing up to the ceiling. Then she did the same with the other leg. The blocks didn't wobble like Lindsay's arms, so she was able to start straightening her legs. But she didn't get far before she couldn't hold them up any more. This was going to be harder work than she'd ever imagined.

Clare sent Lindsay to work on her somersaults on the trampoline. It was going to be a long time until Tara was ready to try the balance on her partner's hands.

After some practice, Tara managed to get her legs straight in a straddle position, but that *still* wasn't right. Her feet were pointing downwards. Clare said her legs should be parallel to the floor, even pointing slightly upwards. They should never point down towards the floor.

"Think of it as if you're trying to balance something on each leg without it rolling off onto the floor," advised Clare.

Tara tried again. "I can't," she sighed, landing back on the floor.

"It's mainly strength in your arms and legs that you need," said Clare. "If you keep practising for long enough you'll get there."

At the end of Sunday's training session Tara spent some more time working on the blocks, and Clare made Lindsay practise balancing weights on her hands so that she could build up strength too. The rest of their routine was coming together well, but Tara felt like it was nothing without the straddle lever balance.

"It's so *hard*," she sighed, rubbing her sore hands together. Lindsay gave her a sympathetic look. But Sam had heard, too.

"We're working towards a National competition," she said. "Of course it's hard! Just because you won gold at Regionals, that doesn't mean you can stop working. *Anyone* who's ever done a competition knows that!"

She turned and walked off before anyone could say anything. Tara stared at the back of the older girl's pink and purple leotard. Sam seemed to have had it in for her ever since Clare had asked Tara to join the Acro squad, and Tara had no idea why. But Sam had been almost nice since the Regional competition. Now it looked like it didn't take much for her to start being nasty again.

"Shall we go through the routine?" Lindsay asked, knowing that would make Tara forget about Sam.

Tara shook her head and glared at the wooden blocks. "We're going to get this balance," she said.

Tara was working so hard that she didn't notice when the others wandered out to the changing room at the end of the session.

"Your dad phoned," Clare said, coming up behind her. "He said he's stuck in traffic so he'll be a bit late."

"Okay." Tara smiled, glad of the chance to practise for a bit longer. She picked the wooden blocks up and moved into one corner of the floor, so that she could carry on working while another group of gymnasts used the rest of the space.

"Home time, Tara!" she heard Dad call a little later. She came down from a neat straddle lever balance and grinned at him.

"Did you see that?" she asked excitedly. "That was my best one yet!"

"Looked great," said Dad. "I've been watching you for a while – it looks difficult! Go and get your things now, Mum's doing a roast dinner."

In the car on the way home, Dad quizzed Tara about what she'd been doing and what she needed to use the blocks for. She explained the balance and how the blocks were easier to start learning it with and would help her build up strength. She was really glad that Dad was so interested, but couldn't help giggling when he kept getting all the names of the skills wrong.

"Mum and I thought it would be nice to go for a family walk after lunch," said Dad. "Have you got much homework to do?"

"Quite a lot." Tara grimaced. She still had some left from during the week, as well as the things she'd been set on Friday. "And I'm going round to Kate's at six to watch a film."

Dad frowned. "Why didn't you do it yesterday?"

"I did some, but they've given us loads and loads this week, Dad." Tara didn't mention that she should have done most of it on Wednesday. With two hours in the gym straight after a whole day at school, she'd been exhausted when she got home and homework hadn't even crossed her mind. Dad would probably understand that, she thought, but for some reason she still didn't tell him. Parents got funny about things like homework. It was better to let them think it was all under control.

Chapter Six

When Mum heard how much work Tara had to do, she decided that going for a walk wasn't such a good idea. So there was just enough time for Tara to dash through her homework before going over to Kate's house.

"Did you finish all that homework?" Mum asked, while she was driving Tara over to Kate's. "I'm worried that all this gymnastics and so much schoolwork is going to get too much for you.

Are you sure you'll be able to cope with it?"

"*Yes,*" Tara said, rolling her eyes and wishing Mum hadn't asked. She knew that she hadn't done any of the homework as well as she could have done if she'd spent more time on it, but she tried to push that thought out of her mind and focus on enjoying a film with her friends.

But even at Kate's she couldn't escape the subject of homework.

"Did you write up our science experiment?" Emily asked, while Kate was tipping popcorn into a bowl.

"Yeah, this afternoon," Tara replied. "How much did you write for each section?"

"About half a page," said Emily, taking a few pieces of popcorn. "I didn't know how much we were meant to do."

"Me neither," Tara agreed. She bit her lip worriedly – she'd only written a couple of sentences about each part of the experiment.

✻ ✻ ✻

When she got home from school on Monday, she went straight up to her room, determined to spend more time on homework and do it all properly this week. She got out her geography book and put it on her desk. She was just about to start answering the questions they'd been set when she noticed a scrap of paper she'd been doodling gymnasts on the day before, and she started to daydream. She pictured herself at the Nationals: a huge gym with a cheering crowd, all watching as she and Lindsay performed a perfect routine packed with stunning balances...

She knew her daydreams would never come true if she didn't keep training hard. She'd have to wait until Wednesday to practise straddle levers on the wooden blocks again, but she was desperate to keep improving even on days when she couldn't go to the gym. She looked at her watch; it was still early. A little bit of stretching wouldn't take too long...

After her usual stretches, Tara couldn't resist

practising a few handstands in the middle of the room, counting how long she could hold them before she had to come down. Trying not to make any noise made it harder – she didn't want to disturb her parents downstairs. Then she remembered that Clare had said she could try building up strength in her arms and wrists by practising straddle levers on the floor. She got into position and gave it her best, but it was much harder than on the blocks.

After a while, Tara sat in the middle of her bedroom floor, gazing at the posters of gymnasts she'd put up on the walls. She wondered if they'd practised in their bedrooms, too. She smiled up at the poster of Beth Tweddle flying between the asymmetric bars. Tara wondered how many hours of training champion gymnasts like Beth had to do to be that good. A lot more than eight hours a week, she bet.

After dinner, she watched TV with Anna for a while.

"Have you done your homework, Tara?" asked Mum, while Dad was clearing up in the kitchen.

"I don't have any today," Tara lied. The truth was that, as well as geography, she had some science questions and another one of Mr. Bruce's history research tasks, but none of it was due in the next day. The science could wait until tomorrow, and the history wasn't due in until next week, so she could leave it for the weekend if she wanted to. Mum would only nag if she knew Tara was putting it off. So even though she felt a bit guilty, it was easier to pretend.

Even though she'd planned to get the science questions done on Tuesday evening, it was harder to fit in than Tara had thought. First of all, her bus home got stuck in traffic and she had to sit there for ages while the minutes ticked away, taking her chance to get everything done with them. It was actually quite fun being stuck on the bus with loads of people from school (especially because she and Emily had been lucky enough to get seats) – someone was playing music on their phone, and everyone was talking and laughing. But although Tara joined in, she couldn't get rid of the little homework worry in the back of her mind.

When she finally got home, she stood in the kitchen chatting to Mum and telling her all about school, helping to grate cheese and chop vegetables for a pasta bake while she talked. Dad came home from work and told them all funny stories from his day while they ate dinner. Tara asked him lots of questions, trying to keep him talking. She didn't want anyone to ask about her homework.

Eventually, she had no other choice. The pasta bake had been eaten, and the plates cleared away. Tara went up to her room and started the maths homework Mr. Spencer had given them, which they had to give back to him the next day. It took longer than she'd thought it would, especially when she gave herself a little break to do some stretches. She'd just sat back down at her desk to start on the science questions when Mum knocked on her door and came in.

"Stop working now," she said. "It's time for bed."

"But I've got to finish this," Tara protested.

"You need to sleep or you'll be too tired for school and gymnastics tomorrow," said Mum. Tara nodded and put her book away – being too tired to train properly at Silverdale was unthinkable. "Goodnight," said Mum, giving her a kiss.

"Night," mumbled Tara. She got ready for bed and tried to sleep. But she couldn't stop thinking about her homework – she was supposed to hand the science questions in the next morning! For the first time in her life, Tara had not done her homework on time, and she knew she was going to be in trouble.

On the way to school on Wednesday, she thought of a way to avoid that. She hadn't done the science questions, but she knew Emily had. Her best friend had done them on Monday night, and she'd said they were easy but long. There wouldn't be time to actually do the questions before she had to hand them in...but there *would* be time to copy Emily's.

Tara waited anxiously at the school gate for her best friends. She had her rucksack on her back and her gym bag slung over her shoulder – she had training straight after school so she'd had to bring her leotard with her. Lindsay and Megan went to Tara's school too – they were in Year Nine – so the three of them always walked to the gym together on Wednesdays and Fridays. It was one of Tara's favourite times of the week – walking along with her gym friends, knowing that school was finished for the day and they were on their way to two whole hours of gymnastics.

"Hi," said Kate, coming up to Tara with a wave and a smile.

"Where's Em?" asked Tara. "She wasn't on my bus."

"She texted me to say she missed it," said Kate. "Her dad's giving her a lift."

Tara looked at her phone and saw she had the same message. "Come on, Emily," she muttered.

"What's the matter?" asked Kate.

Tara didn't have time to answer, because at that moment Emily rushed up to them, out of breath. "My stupid brothers made me miss the bus," she said, already walking ahead. "Come on, we'll be late."

"Em," said Tara, catching up with her. "You know those science questions?"

"Yeah?"

"Um…" Tara paused. Suddenly she realized that Emily might not want her to copy her homework. After all, Emily had worked hard on it. It wasn't fair that Tara could do nothing and get the same mark.

"Please tell me you've done them," said Emily. "I've heard Mrs. Long gives out detentions for the tiniest thing. After-school ones, sometimes."

Tara swallowed. She couldn't have detention after school. Not today. "Of course," she said quickly. "I just wanted to check something. The last ones were a bit confusing."

Emily looked at her strangely. Tara bit her lip. "Sure," said Emily. She looked in her school bag and pulled out her science book. "Take it and give it back to me in the lesson. We're going to miss registration if we don't hurry."

"Thanks," Tara said.

When Tara got to her form room she found out that Mrs. James, her form teacher, was running late – which meant that she had time to copy Emily's answers onto her own worksheet before her teacher arrived. Then she shoved her book back into her bag along with Emily's and sat quietly waiting for the register. She could see two of the boys in her form copying the science answers from someone else's book too. Perhaps that should have made her feel better... But it didn't.

When she arrived at the science block later, she handed Emily's book back to her without a word. She felt sick – she couldn't even look at her best friend. But it was done now. When Mrs. Long collected in their books, Tara was sure she'd somehow be caught out. But nothing happened. Her book went into the pile with all the others, just as if she had done the homework properly. *It's surprisingly easy to get away with it*, Tara thought. Though she felt so guilty that she vowed she'd never do it again.

Chapter Seven

On Friday, Mr. Spencer gave them fifty maths questions to do over the weekend. The class groaned.

"That's going to take for ever!" said Alex, the boy who sat next to Tara.

Tara nodded, worried. She had geography and history homework to do as well. She definitely didn't have for ever to do it all in as she had gym after school that night, and then on Saturday morning and again on Sunday. When she added in Sunday lunch at Auntie Hazel's, and hanging out with Emily and Kate on Sunday night, she was left with only a few hours to do all that homework.

She was quiet on the way to the gym with Lindsay and Megan, still trying to figure out how she could fit everything in. But as soon as she walked through the doors at Silverdale, her worries disappeared and she thought only about gymnastics. She loved the way the gym could make her forget about everything else.

She was getting pretty good at backflips now, and Clare had finally agreed to put one in Tara and Lindsay's Nationals routine. She was also getting better at straddle levers on the blocks, so she and Lindsay had decided to try the full balance again. And this time, for a split second, they managed to get it right. Tara felt her heart bounce in excitement. They could do it! An image flashed through her mind: herself and Lindsay at the

Nationals, wowing the audience with a steady straddle lever balance.

Then they fell. Tara just wasn't strong enough to hold the balance for more than a second.

"So close!" said Clare. "Keep working on the blocks," she told Tara. "You're really nearly there."

Tara grinned and got back to work. All that practising in her bedroom had been worth it!

Clare was also teaching Tara to do a round-off straight into a backflip. It was the basic beginning of tumble runs that Tara had seen Olympic gymnasts doing, and she couldn't believe she was finally doing it herself. Of course, the great champion gymnasts followed their round-off flicks with somersaults – doubles and triples and sometimes with twists. Tara hoped she had that to look forward to one day.

Tara left the gym on Saturday after another great training session. She was finally beginning to feel like a National medal might actually be *just* within her reach.

"I've got a surprise for you," said Dad, as soon as Tara and Mum got back from Silverdale.

"What is it?" Tara asked.

"Close your eyes." She did, leaning against the kitchen counter, and kept them closed while she heard the back door open. Something knocked against the tiled floor. "Okay, open!" said Dad, and Tara's eyelids flew up.

"Wow!" she gasped. "Where did you get it?" On the kitchen floor was a set of wooden blocks, just like the one she used at Silverdale.

"I made it," said Dad. "I thought you'd like to practise your stuff at home."

"Thanks! It's great," said Tara. She ran her fingertips over the smooth blocks. She put her hands on them and tried leaning over so that the blocks took most of her weight. She grinned up at Dad, then leaped over the blocks to give him a big hug.

Handsprings and Homework

"Go on then," he said. "Show me what you can do."

Tara showed him a pretty good straddle lever. "Can I take it up to my room?" she asked.

"I think that's best," said Dad. "It'll get in the way down here. But no gymnastics tricks in the middle of the night. Gymnasts need their sleep."

"Dad!" she laughed, rolling her eyes. "They're not called *tricks*!" He looked at her seriously. "I won't use it at night. Promise."

"And not until all your homework is done," added Mum.

"Okay," said Tara, as usual throwing her eyes up to the ceiling at the mention of homework.

She set the blocks down in the middle of her bedroom floor. She'd rushed through her history homework after gym on Friday but her geography and maths books still sat, untouched, on her desk. But Clare had told her to keep working on the straddle lever. That was a bit like homework, too – and she should really try out her new blocks properly. Just a few minutes of practising and then she'd get on with the boring geography questions...

But when Tara got stuck into training, a few minutes could turn into an hour. Her straddle levers were starting to feel great. She was *so close* to being able to hold the full balance with Lindsay, and she was determined to push herself more than ever until they could do it.

Worn out and hands aching, Tara eventually sat down at her desk and opened her geography book. She knew the maths would take ages, so she rushed through the geography questions and moved on to Mr. Spencer's worksheet. But she only got halfway through before she gave up. It was time for dinner and she was exhausted.

After the competition training session on Sunday morning, Tara changed into jeans and a pretty pink top instead of just pulling comfy clothes on over her favourite black leotard with silver sparkles as usual. She pulled her messy blonde hair out of its ponytail and quickly brushed it. Even though it was the end of January and it was cold outside, the gymnasts had been working hard in the gym and Tara felt hot and sweaty as she hurried to put her leotard and tracksuit away in her bag. Mum, Dad and Anna would be waiting for her in the car park so that they could all go to Auntie Hazel's house.

Outside, the freezing air was refreshing.

"Have a good afternoon!" called Lindsay, heading for her dad's car.

"Maybe see you at school tomorrow," replied Tara. Suddenly she froze on the spot. School was *tomorrow* – and she still hadn't finished that maths homework! Lunch with Auntie Hazel would take all afternoon, and then Emily and Kate were coming over to watch a DVD. How was she *ever* going to get all her homework done?

"Emily!" Tara cried on Monday morning, seeing

her friend standing by the school gate. "I need to ask you for something. A *massive* favour."

"Sure," said Emily. "What do you want?"

Tara took a deep breath. "I need to copy your maths homework."

"*What?*" gasped Emily. "But last night you said you'd done it."

"I don't want to copy all of it…"

"Why didn't you do it?" Emily asked. Her blue eyes were wide with worry.

"I started it," said Tara, "but I didn't have time to finish. There was so much, and I had geography and history to do too. *Please*, Emily," she begged. "I *really* don't want to get into trouble with Mr. Spencer." Emily didn't say anything. "Are you mad at me?" asked Tara.

"No," said Emily. Tara could almost see the thoughts going round and round in her friend's head. "No, of course I'm not mad," Emily said suddenly, more like her usual self again. "It's no big deal. I've seen other people copying homework.

I just never thought..." She didn't finish. She dug around in her bag for her maths book. "Tara... maybe...do you think you're spending too much time doing gym?"

"Don't worry so much, Em!" said Tara. "I'm fine. It's been a bit busy but everything's under control."

"Okay," said Emily, holding her book out to Tara. She still sounded a bit unsure – although whether about letting Tara copy her work, or whether things really were under control, Tara couldn't tell. "I don't know if all the answers are right. Probably not."

Tara hesitated. "Are you sure you don't mind?"

Emily hesitated too. "It's fine," she said finally. "It's just homework. I don't want you to get into trouble either."

"Thank you so *much*," said Tara. She shoved the book into her bag, looking around to see if anyone was watching. She felt like she and Emily were doing something illegal. "I promise I won't do this again."

Emily didn't reply; she just looked worried.

Chapter Eight

On Wednesday, Tara sat in her geography lesson thinking about the Nationals. Mrs. James was handing back the class's books with the previous week's homework. Tara's book slapped down onto the table, breaking her out of her daydream. She flipped the pages until she came to the last one she'd used. There was red writing all over it. *See me*, it said at the bottom. She glanced at Kate's page, which was covered by neat handwriting and pretty red ticks. Tara waited while Mrs. James explained the task for the lesson and handed round some pictures to look at. Then she got up and took her book to the teacher's desk.

"Tara," sighed Mrs. James. She pointed at Tara's open book. "This isn't good enough. I know you can do better."

"Sorry," Tara said quietly.

"How long did you spend on this?" asked Mrs. James. Tara was silent. Not long enough, she knew. Mrs. James sighed again. "I know you all like to go out and have fun at the weekends—" she began.

"It wasn't that!" Tara interrupted. "I had gymnastics both mornings, and loads of maths and history homework too."

Mrs. James raised her eyebrows. "You do a lot of gymnastics, don't you?" she commented. Tara remembered that she'd talked about doing gym on her first day in Year Seven, when Mrs. James had got her form to tell everyone a bit about themselves. "Just make sure it doesn't get in the way of your schoolwork," she continued. Tara fiddled with the pink beads on the bracelet Kate had made her for Christmas. She nodded uncertainly. What could she do? It wasn't as if she could just stop going to Silverdale and she didn't think she'd spent *that* much time at home doing gym... "Go and sit down then," said Mrs. James. Tara went back to her seat and miserably wrote the date at the top of the next page.

Kate raised her head from her work and looked at Tara, full of silent questions. Matt grimaced and rolled his eyes, as if to say *Teachers! Always complaining about something!* It was meant to make Tara laugh...but it didn't. She'd never been told that her work wasn't good enough before.

Maths was later, and it was worse. Mr. Spencer gave the class's books to Alex, and he went around the room, handing them out and chatting. It gave the rest of the class time to chat, too. Tara had turned round in her seat and was talking to the girl who sat behind her when she heard someone come up to her table.

"Tara, can I speak to you for a minute?" asked Mr. Spencer. Tara looked up at him, alarmed. Her hands went suddenly cold. She got up and went to the teacher's desk, expecting him to follow. He didn't. When she turned to look, he was standing by Emily and Kate's table, and Emily looked just as worried as Tara. Emily stood up and came to the front of the room, followed by Mr. Spencer. Tara glanced at his desk. Her maths book was open at the page where she'd copied Emily's homework. Emily's book was open, too. Tara closed her eyes. She'd been caught.

"Did you two do the homework together?" Mr. Spencer asked them.

"No," Tara whispered.

"You've made a lot of the same mistakes," the teacher said. He looked at them each for a long moment.

"It's not Emily's fault!" Tara said. Her voice cracked on the first word.

Mr. Spencer crossed his arms and looked at Tara. "What's not Emily's fault?" he asked.

"I copied some of the questions," Tara admitted. "I...I hadn't finished and I..." She started to mumble, embarrassed. "I was scared of getting in trouble."

"You can sit down, Emily," said Mr. Spencer. Emily took her maths book from the desk and looked worriedly at Tara as she went back to her seat.

"Now, Tara," Mr. Spencer continued. Tara was glad that their maths class was a noisy group. She hoped all the chatter would cover the sound of Mr. Spencer telling her off. "Can you tell me why you didn't finish? Was it too difficult? You know that you can come and ask me for help."

"No, it wasn't that..." said Tara. "I just didn't have time."

"I see." Mr. Spencer's expression changed from kindness to a stern frown.

"Because of gymnastics," Tara explained. He probably thought she'd decided to go shopping or to the cinema or something instead of doing her homework. She had to make him see that it wasn't like that at all. "I'm training for a big competition so there are extra sessions at weekends."

"Well," said Mr. Spencer, "if you're not able to keep up in school, maybe you need to think about giving up gymnastics. I'm going to have to mention this to your form teacher, and it's up to her whether she takes it any further. If this happens again, we'll have to speak to your parents. You can stay in at lunchtime and do some more questions on percentages. You won't learn how to do this by yourself if you just copy the answers from your friends."

Tara went back to her seat. She felt angry for a second, but then she was ashamed. Mr. Spencer was right to give her detention. She had cheated on the homework, after all, even though she *could* have done the questions by herself. At least she didn't have to stay behind after school to do it, so she was saved from having to miss training at Silverdale. At the thought of Silverdale, she remembered what Mr. Spencer had said – he couldn't *really* think she should give up gym to concentrate on school stuff, could he? *Well, so what?* thought Tara. Teachers didn't have the power to stop her doing gymnastics.

But he *could* tell Mum and Dad that it was getting in the way of her schoolwork, she realized. And if that happened, would Mum and Dad still think gymnastics was a great idea?

"Are you okay?" asked Alex.

Tara nodded, hardly even hearing him. If Mr. Spencer or Mrs. James spoke to Mum and Dad, they might decide she had to stop going to Silverdale. No more Nationals. No more Acro. No more Clare, or Lindsay, or all that wonderful equipment. She *couldn't* go back to practising by herself in the garden. Her eyes filled with tears just at the thought of it.

Chapter Nine

The most wonderful thing about gymnastics, Tara thought, was that it could instantly make everything better, even if it was only for a little while. Tara and Lindsay tried the straddle lever balance again that afternoon. It didn't come immediately. The first few tries were almost as bad as when they'd first started learning it. As soon as Tara took her feet off the floor, she went tumbling down to one side. But once they got into it, the balance started to come more easily. Half an hour and countless attempts later, when Tara's leotard was sticking to her back with sweat, they held the balance well for four whole seconds. Then Tara brought herself neatly down to stand on the floor behind Lindsay's head, back in her starting position, still gripping Lindsay's hands. She grinned down at Lindsay, who was laughing up at her from her position on the floor. Tara swung Lindsay's arms back and forth excitedly.

"Nationals here we come!" said Lindsay. The others, who'd been secretly watching while they worked, clapped and cheered. Then it was straight back to work.

By the end of the session, they'd really got it, and Tara felt like anything was possible. She couldn't wait to tell Mum and Dad about it!

"How was school?" asked Mum, as soon as Tara got home from Silverdale that evening. Lindsay's mum had driven her home.

"Okay." Tara shrugged, disappointed that Mum hadn't asked about gym. There was no way she was telling her what had happened in the maths lesson. Maybe if she did her homework really well for the next few weeks, Mr. Spencer wouldn't tell either.

"Have you got any homework?" Mum asked, while she was setting the table for dinner.

Tara frowned, kicking her shoes off and dumping her school bag on the kitchen floor. "Some English," she said, and then scowled even more. "And some French questions I've got to give in tomorrow."

"Tomorrow?" Mum sounded surprised. "They don't usually ask for something in the next day."

"It was set on Monday," Tara told her guiltily.

"I've done my homework," Anna said proudly.

"Yours was only a bit of reading," said Tara. "Wait until you get proper homework, then you won't want to do it so much."

"I thought you liked French," said Mum.

"It's alright," said Tara. "But I'd much prefer to get homework from Silverdale!"

"I bet you would," laughed Mum. "And I bet I'd never have to nag you to get on with it."

Tara smiled, but she couldn't help worrying about what Mum would think if Mr. Spencer told her she'd copied Emily's work. Feelings of guilt crept over her again, so she grabbed her school bag and ran upstairs, away from Mum and Anna. She was afraid they'd guess that something was wrong.

She changed quickly out of her navy blue and grey school uniform, which she had put back on after gym, and into a pair of jeans and a cosy green jumper. She set her French exercise book and textbook out on her desk, all ready to go as soon as she'd finished eating dinner.

When they sat down to eat, Anna chatted on and on about her day at school. Tara let her talk. She definitely didn't want to tell everyone about her own day, and she didn't want anyone to bring up homework again.

As soon as dinner was over, she went back upstairs and sat down at her desk, but the blocks caught her eye and she couldn't resist. Doing the balance on Lindsay's hands had felt so good, and she wanted to get that feeling back. Worrying about homework and Mr. Spencer and being in trouble for copying felt *horrible*. She knew that a few minutes on the blocks would help…

The next thing Tara heard was Anna saying goodnight and going to bed. She looked at the clock. It was 8 p.m. already! She still hadn't even taken her pencil case out of her bag. Mum knocked on her bedroom door.

"Watch this," Tara said grinning, when Mum opened the door. She performed her best straddle lever.

"Brilliant!" said Mum. "Did you get all that homework done?"

"Oh, um…yes."

"Good," said Mum. "How about you stop working hard for the evening and come and watch a bit of telly with me before bed?"

Tara couldn't admit that she hadn't really done her homework. She had no choice but to follow Mum downstairs, desperately trying to figure out when she was going to do those French questions. Maybe if she got up really early the next morning...

Chapter Ten

But the next morning there wasn't time. She was kept awake all night by worried thoughts, and when she finally got to sleep, she was so tired that she slept right through the extra-early alarm she'd set. In fact, she didn't wake up until Mum called her. She got dressed and ate breakfast as fast as she could, but she didn't have time to do even one question before she had to leave to catch her bus. She knew she wouldn't even be able to do the work at break, or lunch, because French was the first lesson of the day. Maybe her French teacher would forget to ask for their books. All she could do was cross her fingers and hope.

There was no chance to rush through the questions in her form room during registration either, because they had to go straight to a big assembly for all of Year Seven, Eight and Nine. Tara caught sight of Lindsay and Megan sitting with the other Year Nines. They smiled at her and Lindsay waved, but Tara was too worried to do anything except smile quickly back and look out for Miss Carter sitting with the other teachers. Her last hope was that the French teacher might be out of school today.

That hope didn't last long. She spotted Miss Carter, and then saw that Mrs. James was sitting next to Mr. Spencer, talking quietly and looking concerned. Tara swallowed. Was Mr. Spencer telling Mrs. James about Tara copying Emily's maths homework?

Assembly went on longer than it should have done. When they were finally released from the hall, everyone rushed off to their first lesson. Tara hurried along the corridor with Kate, but inside all she wanted was to slow right down and never get there.

Miss Carter didn't ask for their homework straight away. They learned the names of different foods and then spent the rest of the lesson in pairs, pretending to order things in a cafe. By the time the bell rang, Tara felt much more relaxed. She'd almost forgotten about the homework, and the class immediately started putting away books and pencil cases.

"Not so fast!" called Miss Carter. "Pass your books to the front, please."

Tara felt her stomach plummet down to her feet. Everyone began to pass their blue French exercise books forward to the person sitting in front of them. Matt, in front of Tara, looked back at her, holding out his hand. She quickly shook her head, and he shrugged, turning back to the front.

When the books were piled on Miss Carter's desk, she counted them. Then she frowned and went through them more slowly, looking up at the class every few seconds to check names against people. Finally she raised her head again, looking straight into Tara's anxious brown eyes. Tara's heart beat as fast as if she'd just taken a big run-up on the tumble track and flown into a handspring.

"Where's your book, Tara?" asked Miss Carter.

Tara swallowed. "I haven't done the questions," she said. She could feel twenty-seven pairs of eyes staring at her.

"I see," said the teacher. "You can all go," she said to the rest of the class. "Tara, we'll talk about this at break time. Go along to your next lesson now."

Tara gratefully got up and hurried out of the classroom, where Kate was waiting for her after her English lesson in the room next door.

Tara barely heard Kate's chatter as they walked towards their next classrooms. There were too many silent questions going round in her own head. Was Miss Carter going to tell Mrs. James? Tara had already had detention for copying Emily's maths homework, and she guessed that Mrs. James knew about that now. What was going to happen this time?

Music was next, but Tara barely heard any of the lesson and she spoke as little as she could get away with. In less than an hour she was going to find out how much trouble she was in. She was afraid she was going to cry.

At break time, she forced herself to go back to Miss Carter's classroom. Mrs. James was there too, sitting at her desk with a mug of tea.

"Um...hi..." Tara said quietly. Mrs. James looked up and put down her pink and white polka-dot mug.

"Come and sit down," Miss Carter said, getting up and pulling a chair from the front row up to her own desk.

Tara sat on the edge of it, pushing her hands underneath her legs so that she was sitting on them and couldn't fiddle nervously with her school skirt.

"Now," said Miss Carter in a kind voice, "can you tell me why you didn't do the questions I gave you?"

Tara thought about saying she'd tried and found the homework too difficult, but she'd already lied to Mum about it. She didn't want to lie to Mrs. James and Miss Carter too. "I...they were...I didn't have time."

"Why not?" asked Miss Carter.

"I was practising gymnastics," Tara said eventually.

Mrs. James sighed. "I thought that might be it. You're in a National competition soon, aren't you?"

Tara nodded.

"That's great," said Mrs. James. "We have a few other gymnasts at Hollypark."

"Lindsay and Megan," said Tara.

"Yes, I've taught both of them," said Mrs. James. "And others, too. But, Tara, you mustn't let gymnastics get in the way of your schoolwork. They've all had to learn that, and you need to as well. I've had reports from some of your teachers that they're worried about how you're doing in their classes, and so am I. Sports and clubs outside school are no excuse to skip your homework, no matter how important your competition is. And copying someone else's work is something I just can't accept."

Tara looked down at her feet, feeling tears welling up in her eyes. Her cheeks were burning and she knew she'd gone bright red. "I'm sorry," she said, without looking up.

"I'm afraid I'm going to have to let your parents know what's happening – I'll be speaking to them this afternoon." Tara jerked her head up, a look of panic on her face. "I'm not calling them so that they can tell you off, or because I'm angry with you. I'm worried that you're going to fall behind, and I think it would help you if your parents know you're struggling. They should be able to help you to fit homework in as well as gymnastics."

"Please don't tell them I should stop doing gym!" begged Tara.

"I'm not going to tell them that," said Mrs. James. "Though it may be something that you should talk about with them."

"What?" Tara whispered.

"It's very difficult to balance sports training with schoolwork," said her teacher. "If you're not able to manage it, I'm afraid that schoolwork has to come first."

The bell rang for the end of break. Tara got up and somehow found her way to her next class. At lunchtime, Kate and Emily tried to find out what had happened but Tara was so upset that her explanation didn't make much sense.

The rest of the day passed in a daze. If someone

had asked her at the end of the day what lessons she'd had after lunch, she wouldn't have been able to tell them. She got the bus home automatically, her feet doing all the moving for her. She felt worse and worse the closer she got to home.

When she got to her front door, she stopped. Her key was in her hand, but she wanted to wait a little longer. She felt distraught and ashamed – she'd lied to Mum about her homework, and by now her parents would know. They'd probably heard all about her copying Emily's work, too, and she knew they'd be disappointed in her. Her greatest fear was that they'd be so disappointed that they'd pull her out of the Nationals. Because if that happened, her whole world would fall apart.

Chapter Eleven

"Tara, come in here!" Mum called from the living room, as soon as Tara closed the front door behind her.

"Hi, Mum," she said, slowly walking into the room.

Mum was sitting in an armchair. "I had a phone call from your form teacher just now," she said. "Mrs. James." Tara nodded silently. "Oh, Tara..." said Mum. "I did worry that all this gymnastics was going to be too much for you."

"It's not too much!" Tara cried.

"Well, something's obviously too much," said Mum. "You can't just stop doing your homework."

"I'm sorry," Tara said, going over to Mum. She kneeled on the floor by Mum's chair. "I'm so, so sorry and I'll never skip homework again. *Please* don't make me stop going to Silverdale!"

Mum sighed. "I don't want to. I know how much you love it, and I've seen how good you are at gymnastics. We're so proud of you for that. But we've always been proud of you for doing well at school, too."

"But school's different," said Tara. "Everyone goes to school. Not everyone has a chance to be a National champion. But *I've* got that chance now. I probably won't win, and maybe I'll never be a World Champion or a real gymnastics star but, *please*, you've got to let me *try!*"

"School is important too, Tara. I'll talk about it with Dad when he gets home. How about you go and get started on your homework? We all know how hard you work at gym, but you need to show everyone you can work hard at school, too." She paused. "I'm sorry, Tara, but if you can't keep up, I think you'll have to leave Silverdale."

Tara silently went upstairs and got out her science book. She'd hardly paid any attention in the lesson that afternoon, so the homework was a mystery to her. She stared at it for a while. Then the bang of the front door closing made her jump. Dad was home.

"Evening all!" she heard him call. Without even seeing him, she knew he was hanging up his coat and putting his shoes neatly on the shoe rack before going into the kitchen to see Mum and Anna. She decided to stay upstairs. Dad sounded happy. But in a few minutes, Mum was going to tell him about Mrs. James's phone call and the homework, and then he was going to be disappointed and upset. Tara didn't want to see that. Instead, she sat on her bed with her feet curled up underneath her and called Emily. She pressed the phone to her ear while it rang, as if that would somehow make Emily be right there with her.

"Hey," said Emily, answering the phone after a few rings. "What happened with your parents?"

"They're talking now," Tara said miserably. She could hear a familiar voice in the background.

"It's Tara," said Emily, her voice sounding quiet as if she'd turned her head away from her phone.

"Is Kate there?" Tara asked.

"She's helping me babysit my brothers," said Emily. "I would have asked you, too, but I know you don't have time with homework and... everything."

"So what did your mum say?" asked Kate, loudly enough for Tara to hear her while Emily put her phone onto the speakerphone setting.

"That she doesn't want to make me stop doing gym but homework's important," said Tara.

Handsprings and Homework

"I can't understand how you could just *not do* homework," said Emily.

"I can," said Kate. "That French homework was *boring!*"

"But *you* still did it," argued Emily. "Tara, you could get in real trouble if you keep putting gymnastics first."

"I'm already in trouble," said Tara. "But there's *no way* they're taking Silverdale away from me! If I have to keep up with school so that I'm allowed to carry on with gym, then that's what I'll do. It's like another part of training."

"Not everything's part of training!" exclaimed Emily. "Remember when you spent so much time doing gym that you hardly got to see us? Then you realized that you need to do things with friends as well. This is just like that – other parts of life are important, too."

"Like school," added Kate. "Even though it sometimes seems like the worst place ever."

"You're right," sighed Tara. She lay back on the

bed and closed her eyes. Juggling so many things was tiring. "I'd better go," she said. "Time to face the parents."

"Good luck," said Kate.

"It'll be okay," said Emily.

But Tara wasn't so sure.

Everything had gone quiet downstairs. Tara left her room and crept down the stairs until she was sitting on the third one from the bottom. She could hear Mum and Dad talking.

"This is serious!" said Mum. "She copied Emily's homework!"

"Oh, but just once," said Dad. "Don't tell me you never skipped a piece of homework when you were at school, or copied a couple of questions from someone else. She's eleven! It's not like she's cheated on an important exam."

"That's not the point," insisted Mum. "I don't want her to fall behind in school because she's putting all of her time and energy into gymnastics."

"Neither do I," said Dad. "But she *loves* gym. She's happy when she's training, anyone can see that. I'm not going to be the one to take that away from her."

Tara held her breath. She hated that her parents were arguing because of her. But, *Please let Dad win*, she thought, squeezing her hands tightly together. *Please, please, please…*

"I don't want to do that either!" Mum shouted. On the stairs, Tara flinched. "But we have to do something. We can't let things go on as they are. She needs to understand that schoolwork is important."

"I do understand that," Tara said, walking into the room. She couldn't stand listening to any more or letting her mum get any more upset. "I'm going to work really hard at school from now on, and I promise not to practise gym at home until all my homework's finished. Please give me one more chance," she said sincerely.

Mum and Dad looked at each other. "You have to really mean it," said Dad.

"I do," Tara replied earnestly. She could see the faint shimmer of a chance. Silverdale might not be taken away from her just yet. "I'm going to get started on my homework right now. I'll do all of it tonight so it'll be out of the way before gym at the weekend."

"If you're serious about this," said Mum, "then we'll give you a chance to prove yourself."

"Thank you!" Tara cried, hugging Mum and then Dad and then both of them at the same time. "I won't let you down, I promise!"

"Mrs. James is going to call me next week with an update," warned Mum. "So if anything slips, I'm going to know about it."

Tara nodded seriously. The next week was going to put her to the test in a way no gym competition could.

Chapter Twelve

A week later, Mrs. James kept Tara back after her geography lesson. Tara's heart sank. She'd worked harder than ever before at school, and had only spent one hour practising on the blocks when she should have been doing homework. It was so hard to resist when they were sitting there in her room, just begging her to work on straddle levers. Even though she and Lindsay were getting pretty good at the full balance, working on the blocks was still good for keeping up strength and perfecting the straddle position.

"How are you doing?" asked Mrs. James. "I've had good reports from all your teachers."

Tara smiled, relieved. "I'm fine," she said. "Sometimes it's hard to force myself to do homework when all I can think about is training for the competition, but I know I have to do it."

"Working for a National competition must be really exciting!" said Mrs. James. Tara was surprised that she sounded so interested.

So Tara explained everything – all about the Regionals and the Nationals, how exciting it was and how if she didn't manage the straddle lever balance on the day, they didn't even have a shot at gold. She tried to describe what it was like when she really focused, how the time flew by without her even noticing.

"I know what that's like," said Mrs. James. "I used to be a good runner when I was a teenager.

Sometimes when I got home from school, all I wanted to do was go out for a run, but there was always so much homework to do as well."

"Really?" Tara looked at her teacher in a new way. It was weird to think of Mrs. James as a teenager. "What did you do?"

"I tried to be organized, but I wasn't very good at it. I gave up running in the end. To be a true champion, you have to be very disciplined."

"I'm going to be a champion," Tara said. "I *want* to be, anyway. I'll learn to be the most organized person in the world."

"Then I'm sure you'll go far." Mrs. James smiled and looked out of the window.

"I'm sorry about the homework and…the copying," said Tara. "I really am."

Mrs. James looked back at Tara, her expression serious again. "I meant what I said about schoolwork being important. This week you've done well with your homework. Keep it up, and I'll tell your parents that you're doing better."

Tara nodded, determined. At least she could stay at Silverdale for now. She would train hard while she was there, making the most of every second. And she would do all her homework better than ever. They were all going to see that she could manage school *and* gymnastics.

There was still five minutes left of break, so Tara went outside to find her friends. She spotted them on the field, and ran up behind Emily, giving her a big hug.

"Gymnastics is saved?" guessed Emily.

"You were right to tell me how important schoolwork is," said Tara.

"I was just worried."

"You don't have to be any more. I'm going to be as organized as all the great champion gymnasts."

"You'll need to be," said Emily. "Because you're going to be a great champion."

Tara worked hard in lessons and didn't waste time staring out of the window or daydreaming about being at Silverdale. On Wednesdays and Fridays after she, Lindsay and Megan had walked to Silverdale from school, they usually had forty-five minutes to wait until their training session started. Before her talk with Mrs. James, Tara and Lindsay used to spend the time sitting and chatting, or going through their routine. But now Tara quickly changed into her leotard and got her homework out instead. It was amazing how much she could get done now that she was determined to make the wait useful. Over the next few weeks she got into a routine, and found that she didn't mind doing schoolwork instead of chatting if it meant she could keep on top of everything.

"Need some help?" Lindsay asked one afternoon before training started. The competition was less than a month away, but Tara had forgotten all about it for a moment – she was completely focused on her French homework. She stopped chewing the end of her pen and looked up.

"I've forgotten everything we did in the lesson

this morning," she sighed, handing Lindsay the worksheet she had to complete. She had only started learning French that year, and she wasn't very good at it.

"Okay," said Lindsay, reading the sheet of paper quickly. "You need to put the words from this box in the right spaces in the postcard."

"I know, but I can't remember what any of them mean! Why do I need to learn French anyway?" she grumbled.

"What about when you go to international competitions? It could be useful then."

"Good point," said Tara, and grabbed the worksheet back. "Well, I remember *chaud* means hot because Miss Carter said it like she was so boiling hot that she was about to faint."

Lindsay giggled, and then she read some of the other words out and did miming actions to help her partner guess what they meant. By the time Jasmine and Sophie arrived, Tara had finished the worksheet.

Handsprings and Homework

"What subject is it today?" asked Jasmine, dumping her bag on the bench and pulling out a beautiful pale pink leotard with flashes of silver on the sleeves. Tara eyed it enviously for a second. Jasmine had such an amazing collection of leotards. Tara still only had three.

"French." She grimaced. "But it's done now. Lindsay helped me."

Once she'd admitted to them what had happened with her homework, Tara realized that the other gymnasts at Silverdale all understood how difficult it was to keep up with school while training for a National competition. And now that homework was on her mind, she'd noticed that while the others chatted before training, they often worked on school things too, and she knew that Jasmine and Sophie – best friends at school as well as at the gym – did homework together every Saturday afternoon. They were all eager to help if Tara needed it. Jasmine turned out to be really good at maths, and even Sam had chipped in with some advice on history homework.

"Let's forget about homework now," said Megan, suddenly looking up from the pad of paper she was writing on. "It's time for some real work!"

Tara grinned and stuffed the French worksheet and her pencil case in her bag. She grabbed her bottle of water and danced along to the gym with the others.

After the warm-up, they started to work on some tumbling skills. Tara still got a thrill every time she did a round-off flick. It felt great when she and Lindsay did them in time with each other, and she hoped that it looked just as impressive as it felt. She couldn't wait until her parents and Anna saw her and Lindsay performing them in their routine at the Nationals!

Part of her couldn't help worrying though. She was still determined to keep up with her homework, but that meant she couldn't do so much extra practice at home. And the last three weeks until Nationals were the one time when she thought she should be training more than ever. After all, loads of extra practice had helped Lindsay and her to win at Regionals, and the Nationals would be even tougher. Without all the extra practice, she could feel the gold medal she was desperate for slipping further and further from her reach.

Chapter Thirteen

Clare pushed them harder and harder as the competition got closer. By the last week, everyone was getting nervous. No one mentioned their chances at Nationals; none of them wanted to be the one who jinxed it for them all. The competition was on a Saturday and Clare organized an extra-long afternoon training session the day before, which meant the gymnasts had to miss an afternoon of school. When she gave Mrs.

James the note from Mum asking for the time off, Tara had been terrified her form teacher would say no. But Mrs. James had surprised her – not only had she said yes, but she'd asked loads of questions about where the competition was and what it would be like.

If she hadn't been so nervous, Tara might have felt important when she got to walk out of her form room at lunchtime registration that Friday to go to Silverdale. Everyone knew that she was competing the next day, and they all wished her luck.

"Tara doesn't need luck," said Mrs. James. "You've worked hard," her teacher told her. "That's what will earn you that gold medal. You certainly deserve it. I'm very proud of you."

Tara flushed and said a quick "Thanks" before hurrying away. She felt like she might cry, and she couldn't think of *anything* more embarrassing.

Tara walked to the gym with Lindsay and Megan, as usual. The competition was a three-hour drive away and they had to be at the venue early the next morning, hours before the competition actually started, so they were travelling that evening and staying in a bed and breakfast. Their families would travel there on Saturday morning. Mum, Dad and Anna had all given Tara huge hugs that morning before she'd gone to school as she wouldn't get a chance to see them properly again until the competition was over. She shivered slightly. The next time she hugged her parents, either she'd be a National champion...or she wouldn't.

All three girls had bags with their Silverdale leotards and tracksuits, as well as pyjamas and everything they would need to stay overnight. They chattered and laughed all the way to Silverdale, full of energy in the spring sunshine and happy to be out of school early.

The gym was full of nervous excitement when they arrived, but it soon disappeared once they got down to some serious work. They were all far too focused to let nerves take over and stop them from concentrating. Tara and Lindsay went through their routine five perfect times, and it felt incredible.

We're going to do this, Tara suddenly thought, balanced up on Lindsay's shoulders with one leg held high in a Y-balance. *We really could win.*

And then she fell. "Oh no," she groaned.

"What?" demanded Lindsay, thinking the worst. "Are you hurt?"

"No," Tara replied. "Not this again! I thought we'd got this balance sorted." They'd spent so much time working on the straddle lever balance – and it had been worth every second of training, because it looked brilliant now – but what if that meant their other balances weren't good enough?

"Stop," said Lindsay.

"Stop what?"

"Stop *worrying*! We can do the routine. You know we can."

"Lindsay's right," said Clare. "You're tired, and you weren't concentrating. I could see that in your eyes. You'll be fine tomorrow." She looked at the clock. It was nearly four, which meant they'd have to stop working soon. "One more run-through, then go and get changed," she told them. "I don't want you to finish your last training session on a fall. Make your last run-through good, then you'll go into the competition with confidence tomorrow."

Tara and Lindsay nodded and started their routine again, while Clare went off to give Megan and Sophie some last-minute advice.

Tomorrow, echoed in Tara's mind, and she felt a tingle of shivery excitement go down her spine.

Chapter Fourteen

After training, the six girls changed into their own clothes and got into the minibus the club had hired to take them to the competition. Tara sat next to Lindsay, and Sophie sat with Jasmine across the aisle from them. Megan was behind Jasmine and Sam was behind Lindsay, while Clare sat in the front with the driver. As soon as they had all got seated and were on their way, Clare passed them back a bag of sweets. They all got out the sandwiches and drinks they'd brought with them and settled in for a long trip. When Tara opened her lunch box, she found a little note from Mum:

Good luck, Tara! We can't wait to cheer you on. Lots of love, Mum xxxx

She showed it to Lindsay, who smiled, and Tara felt shivers of excitement again. She was on her way to a National gymnastics competition! After all the hard work, she was almost there.

Sam and Megan both had magazines with them, and they whiled away an hour doing quizzes and tests to see which pop stars and film stars they were most like, and which colour nail varnish suited their personalities best. Sophie got out a pack of cards and started to tell everyone's fortunes, but no one asked the only question they really wanted the answer to: would they return to Silverdale as National Champions?

Handsprings and Homework

Tara watched it slowly grow dark outside. Inside the minibus it was warm and they were all tired from the hard afternoon of training. They drifted into quiet murmurs to each other as they chewed the last of the sweets. Tara and Lindsay listened to music together, sharing Lindsay's iPod headphones. With a soundtrack of upbeat music in her ear, Tara looked around at the others. Sam was telling Sophie all the latest gossip from their school. Sophie caught Tara's eye. She gave her a grin, and Tara smiled back. Megan was putting Jasmine's soft black hair into different styles. Jasmine kept trying to turn her head slightly to speak to her, and Megan kept pushing it back around. Tara giggled and leaned against Lindsay's shoulder. Whatever happened tomorrow, she was glad to be here.

It was late when they got to the little bed and breakfast where they were staying for the night. They lugged their bags out of the minibus and trooped inside. Clare spoke to the woman at the desk and sorted out the rooms, while the girls looked around the lobby and peeked through the doors into the rooms on either side. It was a pretty house, with cream walls and a deep red carpet, and vases of flowers on the shelves and tables. They could see a big room with sofas and bookcases on one side of the hall. Tara thought it was a shame they wouldn't really get to see much of the house – they'd be leaving for the competition early the next morning.

They went upstairs and found their rooms. Tara was sharing with Lindsay and Megan, while Jasmine, Sophie and Sam were in the room next door. Clare had the room on the other side of the younger gymnasts.

"We'd better hang our leotards up so they don't get creased," Lindsay suggested, pulling hers out of her bag and smoothing the navy blue velvet.

"Good idea," said Megan. Her own leotard already looked a bit crumpled.

"Hand me yours, Tara, and I'll find some hangers."

Tara carefully lifted her precious Silverdale squad leotard from her bag and gave it to Lindsay. She admired the three navy blue leotards hanging on the front of the wardrobe. They were sleeveless and a white flame shape flickered down from one shoulder. Tara loved how it felt to wear that leotard and know she was part of the Silverdale squad.

"I am *so* tired," yawned Megan, snuggling down in one of the beds.

"I'm setting an alarm for seven," said Lindsay.

"Ugh, don't remind me," groaned Megan. "I could sleep for ever."

"Then you'll sleep right through your chance at gold," giggled Tara.

It was late. Tara couldn't tell *how* late because it was too dark to see her watch. Megan's breathing had evened out into sleep long ago, and Lindsay was lying completely still. Tara was going through the routine in her mind. Suddenly she had a horrible mind-blank. What came after the forward walkover? She searched her brain but couldn't find the answer. Her body knew the routine, she was sure of it – if she could only practise it, she would remember. She sat up and silently slipped out of bed. She moved her bag into the corner as quietly as she could and started to mark through the routine. Lindsay rolled over in her bed and sat up.

"Tara?"

"Sorry," Tara whispered. "I didn't mean to wake you."

"I wasn't asleep. I've been thinking through the routine."

"Me too. I couldn't remember it."

"Let's have one practice together and then go to sleep," whispered Lindsay, joining Tara on the floor.

They were marking through their routine as

quietly as possible, doing the few balances they had space for, and remembering the rest without actually doing it, when they heard a noise outside. Tara came down from the straddle lever balance and held her breath. The door opened.

"What's going on in here?" Clare asked in a low voice.

"Sorry, we were—"

The coach stopped Tara halfway through her explanation. "Girls, I know you're determined to do well tomorrow, but midnight training sessions aren't going to help that. You need to get some sleep."

"We just wanted one last practice," said Lindsay.

"I've seen you two in the gym this week," said Clare, with a smile. "You've done enough." She went out, closing the door silently behind her. Megan was still snoring away in her bed.

Tara thought about what her coach had said as she settled her head on the comfy pillow. They'd done enough. Did that mean that Clare thought…? She stopped herself. She wouldn't even think it. It would be too much like tempting fate. *But, oh,* she thought, *if only it was true!*

Chapter Fifteen

The next morning, after a breakfast of cereal, fruit juice and toast with strawberry jam, they set off in the minibus again. The National Acrobatic Gymnastics Levels 1-4 Competition was being held in a huge sports arena. When they got there, they had to weave their way through a maze of corridors. They followed the crowd of girls and boys dressed in tracksuits, all of them chattering hard in voices loud and high-pitched with nerves.

When they finally entered the arena, Tara's first thought was that she had never seen a gym so massive. There was tiered seating for the audience all the way around, and blue sprung floors had been put down for the gymnasts. Tara looked at the area they would be performing their routine in later and shivered.

"Come on," called Jasmine, walking off arm-in-arm with Sophie. "Let's go and find some space in the warm-up gym." They were already dressed in their Silverdale leotards and tracksuits, and had scraped their hair up into neat buns before they left the bed and breakfast.

Sam led them through a thorough warm-up and then they began to work on their balances. Clare nodded approvingly at Tara, who was high up on Lindsay's shoulders with one leg held in a perfect Y-balance. Competition time was getting closer and closer now, and Tara tried not to think about the judges behind their table, or the other gymnasts in their brightly coloured leotards. She tried to forget about all those seats around the arena and the hundreds of eyes that would be on her, and her parents watching, and Clare and everyone at Silverdale expecting big things… She lowered her leg so she was standing with both feet on Lindsay's shoulders, then took her partner's hands to jump down in front of her, landing with a bit of a wobble.

Suddenly she felt sick. She couldn't do it. She hadn't even been at Silverdale for a year yet – what was she doing at a National competition? There was *no way* she could compete against the other gymnasts here, who had probably all been training since they were tiny. How could she walk out onto that floor, knowing that if she messed anything up, everyone would see that she wasn't the great gymnast she wished she was?

"Come on, it's time to go back into the main gym," Clare said.

Tara followed along behind the others, but she was hardly aware of where she was walking.

She felt small and lost, just like she'd felt on the first day at secondary school. What she wanted more than anything was to run away and go back to doing gymnastics in her back garden.

Tara's nerves and doubts were in danger of taking her over completely… But then the march-in started, and she felt a tiny jolt of excitement return. She couldn't help enjoying the feeling of being a real gymnast while she walked neatly around the floor in a line with all the other competitors. And by the time that had finished, she was actually feeling a bit better.

There were a lot more gymnasts here than there had been at the Regional competition. The Silverdale girls found their place on the benches lining the floor space and waited for everything to start. Tara scanned the tiered seats for her parents' faces, but she couldn't see them – the crowd was just too big.

It wasn't long before the first competition – Level 4 Girls' Pairs – got going, but it would be ages before it was Tara and Lindsay's turn. Watching the other levels compete was making Tara very nervous. They were all good, and not many made mistakes.

"D'you think Jas and Sam are good enough to beat that?" she asked Megan, after a pair of girls had finished a routine packed full of spectacular balances. They were definitely the best so far.

Megan wrinkled her nose in worried thought. "I don't know," she replied honestly. "But their routine is pretty amazing!" They all watched Jasmine and Sam, who were getting ready to perform over on the other side of the floor. They were rubbing chalk on their hands to help them grip and they looked nervous.

"Time to find out," muttered Sophie, as their friends walked out onto the floor.

They all knew the Level 4 pair's routine so well that they noticed instantly when they started a fraction of a second too late. Sophie and Megan looked at each other anxiously. Tara gripped the edge of the bench and leaned forward to watch. Jasmine and Sam performed well, just like they always did, but as the routine went on, their timing slipped a little and Tara realized that they were going to have to make it up somehow. Their routine finished just after a balance – if there wasn't enough music left for them to hold the balance for the full four seconds, they would lose serious marks. Jasmine and Sam obviously realized that too. Seeing a chance to make up a precious second of time, Sam threw Jasmine up into a somersault before she was ready. Jasmine did her best to control her body round in a single somersault instead of a double, but she landed messily. The single somersault would bring their difficulty score down quite a bit, and they'd lose presentation marks for that wobble. Tara covered her face with her hands.

The pair carried on with their routine as if nothing had gone wrong, and performed their finishing balance perfectly. They'd made up the extra second they needed, but it had probably cost them a medal. Tara could hardly look at their faces as they walked off the floor. Their chance was gone and they knew it.

"Sorry, Jas," Sam said quietly, when they'd pulled their tracksuits back on and were sitting with the others.

"Don't be," Jasmine replied sadly. "It's just one of those things."

"At least you didn't fall," Megan added, trying to be helpful.

"There'll be other competitions," said Sophie.

"Easy for you to say," sighed Sam. She leaned back against the wall, staring with empty eyes at the floor, where the Level 4 Boys' Pairs competition had now started. "You've still got *your* chance at gold."

When the scores were in, Sam and Jasmine had come fifth, meaning they didn't get a medal at all.

"Come on, you two," said Clare to Megan and

Sophie, "it's time you went out to the warm-up gym."

"See you later," Megan said, waving to the others as she and Sophie got up.

"Good luck!" said Jasmine warmly. Sam was silent.

As the boys continued to compete on the floor, Tara and Lindsay chatted quietly to two girls on the next bench.

"Your pair would have been brilliant if they hadn't messed up that somersault throw," said one of them, a small girl with long brown hair tied into a plait.

"I know," sighed Tara. "They were trying to make up time because they started a tiny bit late," she explained, realizing that to people who didn't know the routine as well as they did, it probably looked like Sam and Jasmine just couldn't do that throw very well. "If *they* can't win at Nationals I don't know how the rest of us can!"

"What Level are you competing in?" asked the other girl, who was taller. "We're Level 2."

"So are we," said Tara. "I'm Tara and this is Lindsay."

"I'm Josie," said the taller girl.

"I'm Nikki," added the other. "Looks like we'll be competing against you!"

"Bring it on," laughed Lindsay. Tara laughed, too, but the mention of competing made her stomach plummet again.

"Linds!" Jasmine said just then, shaking Lindsay's arm to get her attention. "Megan and Sophie are on!"

Megan and Sophie performed their routine carefully. After what had happened to Sam and Jasmine, they didn't want to let anything go wrong. Clare had given them a routine that showed off their strength and energy, and they put just enough power into it to dazzle the audience, while holding enough back to stay in control. The Silverdale gymnasts all cheered up –

even Sam – when they were given the highest score so far.

Megan high-fived them all when she came back and then watched tensely while the remaining Level 3 pairs performed. Sophie sat completely still on the end of the bench. She hardly even breathed until the last score was up – and they were confirmed as the Level 3 champions! Tara was so excited for them that she almost forgot she still had to face the judges herself.

But during the next round – Level 3 Boys' Pairs – Tara's doubts and worries returned. Her turn was getting closer and closer, and suddenly her eyes filled with tears. She didn't want to mess this up and let Lindsay and Clare down.

Sam noticed that Tara was upset and leaned towards her. "Are you okay?" she asked. "Let's go out to the warm-up gym."

Tara got up uncertainly and followed the older gymnast.

"Tara…" Sam began when they were on their

own, and then she paused. She looked down at her bare feet and scrunched up her toes, scuffing them on the soft blue-carpeted floor. "I know I wasn't very nice to you when you first started..." Tara didn't know what to say. "I'm sorry," Sam blurted out. "I guess I was jealous."

"Jealous?" Tara asked, surprised. "But you're a much better gymnast than me."

Sam shrugged. "It's stupid," she said. "On your first day, I overheard Clare talking to one of the other coaches. She said you were the most promising gymnast she'd seen in a long time."

"What?" gasped Tara. She felt like she was so far behind everyone else. Did Clare really think she had that much talent?

"When we messed up today," said Sam, "I realized that I've been an idiot. I thought I was better than you, but I'm not. I've just been doing gym longer, and I still make mistakes. Anyway, I know your first big competition is really scary, but you've got a chance at gold here and I wanted you to know that Clare believes you can win…and so do I."

Tara couldn't believe it. Sam had been mean because she was jealous. Clare thought she could win. Even *Sam* thought she could win. Tara didn't know *what* she thought herself. "Thanks," she managed to say, finally.

"We'd better go back in," said Sam. "It's your turn soon. Tara, win this for Silverdale."

Tara nodded.

"Here you are!" exclaimed Lindsay, coming into the room. "We've got to start warming up."

"Good luck!" said Sam, heading for the door. Tara smiled.

Lindsay looked at her curiously. "What was that about?" she asked.

"I'll tell you later," Tara replied. Right now they had to focus on the most important performance they'd ever done. And suddenly, instead of dreading it, she couldn't wait.

✷ ✷ ✷

Handsprings and Homework

Tara and Lindsay took their places on the floor. Even though she was still nervous, Tara knew that this was where she was meant to be. They stretched and presented to the judges and then their music started, louder than it had ever sounded before.

These few minutes mattered more than all the hours and hours they had spent working towards them. They began to dance, stepping and jumping lightly into the positions their bodies knew so well. Bouncy handsprings, steady arabesques, a smooth forward walkover... Tara stretched every movement to the limits of what her muscles could do. She felt instinctively that she was perfectly in time with the music and with Lindsay and she knew without looking that their movements matched exactly. The music and the routine swept her towards her partner and she felt as if she almost floated up onto Lindsay's shoulders. She held her head high and her smile sparkled. After a graceful and silent landing on the floor she was off again, twisting and weaving across the floor in a pattern they had worked for hours to create. The straddle lever balance was next.

Tara stood behind Lindsay's up-stretched arms and tried not to think about how impressed her parents would be when they saw her balancing on Lindsay's hands.

Focus, she told herself silently. She took Lindsay's hands, which felt as steady as ever. If Lindsay was nervous about this, she was hiding it well. Tara stretched her legs out, with her feet pointed beautifully. She held the balance, counting slow seconds: one…two…three… As she hit that magic four seconds, she felt like saying "Ta-da!" Instead she grinned and enjoyed the burst of applause. Then she swung back a little to bring her feet down together onto the floor behind Lindsay's head.

They both relaxed a bit after that, and moved smoothly through the rest of the routine: walkovers, the wonderful round-off flick she was so proud of, and a pretty pirouette… Then it was all over. They finished an almost perfect performance, held their last positions for a moment, and then walked off the floor to their tracksuits and a long wait.

"How was it?" Tara asked the others anxiously, brushing chalk from her hands.

"I'd say you're in the running," said Clare. "We'll have to wait and see how the last pairs do."

They didn't have to wait any longer for their own score though. 27.9 put them in the lead so far. Tara gasped. She grinned silently at Lindsay, but didn't want to say anything – they hadn't won yet. She finally spotted her parents near the front in the audience and gave them a wave. They waved back excitedly. Dad looked like he'd never seen anything so brilliant in his whole life, and she was sure she could see Mum brushing a few tears away.

One pair and then another got lower scores than Tara and Lindsay. Josie and Nikki, the final pair, were given 27.7. It was the silver medal score.

Tara leaped up from the bench and clapped her hand over her mouth. She couldn't believe it – she and Lindsay had won! Megan was bouncing up and down on the bench, shaking Lindsay's arm. Sophie and Jasmine got up and hugged Tara at the same time. Sam gave Lindsay a quick hug and then she hugged Tara. Tara and Lindsay could only look at each other in disbelief.

"We did it!" Tara finally said to Lindsay, when their National gold medals had been hung around their necks.

"Well done," said Nikki. "You two deserved to win."

They smiled and chatted with her and Josie while the crowd clapped and cheered for all the medal winners. Megan and Sophie were a little bit further along the floor with their own gold medals.

A man from a newspaper came to take photos of the winners from each level. He also took one of the four Silverdale gold medallists together.

He told them to smile, but there was really no need. They couldn't have stopped grinning even if the end of the world had come.

"Wait," said Tara. "This isn't our whole team." She dashed over to Sam and Jasmine and dragged them onto the floor. "*Now* we're ready!" The photographer took a few more shots.

"You know," said Megan, "it still feels like someone's missing…"

"Clare!" called all six gymnasts at once. Their coach laughed and came over to join them. They could see how pleased she was and it made Tara even happier to know that she had made her coach proud.

After that, they all went off to find their parents.

"You're so cool, Tara!" said Anna. Tara laughed and hugged her little sister.

"We're very proud of you," said Mum. "You did wonderfully! I'd be much too scared to try doing any of those things."

The gymnasts' parents all got cameras out and

the girls stood together for more photos. Tara fingered the gold medal that glittered against her blue and white leotard. She looked down at it shining there and hoped that this feeling would last a long time.

"Eyes up, Tara," said Dad. "There'll be plenty of time for admiring your medal later!"

She smiled for the cameras again, but secretly thought that a smile was not really enough to show how incredibly happy she was. She wanted to dance and jump and turn somersaults! Doing gymnastics was the only way she could possibly express the high she was feeling right now. She couldn't believe that she'd almost let this get taken away from her – this feeling was worth doing all the homework in the world.

Eventually, everyone decided they had taken enough photos and the girls made their way to the car park. All the gymnasts would be going home with their own families, and Clare was getting a lift back with Sam and her dad.

Handsprings and Homework

Tara skipped along beside Lindsay and Megan. "I wonder what we'll be working towards now," she said thoughtfully. Clare had given them a week off to recover from the competition, but soon life at Silverdale would be back to normal.

"There's usually a friendly club competition against Central Gym in June," said Lindsay. "Maybe Clare will enter some of us in that."

"And then there's the summer display, of course," added Tara.

"Clare *promised* Soph and me that we could go to the Elite Training Camp this year," said Megan. "I'm going to start nagging her about it as soon as we're back in the gym!"

"Nag her to let us go as well!" said Lindsay. "It's a week of training at another gym with gymnasts from all over the country. Acro all day, every day!" she explained to Tara.

Tara's whole face lit up. "That sounds amazing!"

Megan nodded. "I've never been but Jasmine said it's brilliant."

They said goodbye to Megan when they reached her mum's car. Tara's family had parked next to Lindsay's parents. They stood by their car doors.

"Bye, Tara," said Lindsay. "Have a good week off."

"You too," Tara said, smiling. "See you back in the gym."

Tara settled into the car, so happy now that she was sure she had years and years to come at Silverdale, with all sorts of competitions and camps and displays ahead of her. Today she was a National Champion, but that was only the beginning of her gym star dreams.

Usborne Quicklinks

For links to websites where you can watch video clips of gymnastics routines and find out more about balances and basic skills and gymnastics organizations, go to the Usborne Quicklinks website at www.usborne.com/quicklinks and enter the keywords "gym stars".

Please read the internet safety guidelines displayed at the Usborne Quicklinks website.

For more dazzling reads head to
www.usborne.com/fiction